The Roman Road

MATT WRIGHT

Illustrations by Claire Zillwood

Wright Way
Publications

*This book is dedicated
to the real Sam and Max,
for walking the Roman Road together.
Remember this is just the beginning!*

ACKNOWLEDGEMENTS

My thanks go to my wife, Rach,
and my friend, Oli, who have helped
to shape the ideas in this book.

Matt Wright

All Scripture quotations are from The Youth Bible.
Copyright © 1993, 2000, 2007 Authentic Media.
© Copyright Matt Wright, Wright Way Publications 2012

If you would like to contact Matt Wright to talk about The Roman Road
or to ask for extra copies please email *jesusistheway@live.co.uk*

British Library Cataloguing in Publication Data.
A catalogue record for this book is available from the British Library.

Publication commissioned by Matt Wright, Wright Way Publications.

ISBN 978 0 86071 6648

Contents

CHAPTER I

A Birthday Present for Sam

Being bullied was nothing strange for Sam. Take now, for instance. He was in the playground being taunted by Andrew and Nash, two bigger boys who often picked on him. They were pushing him around, calling him names and trying to steal his school bag, and the next thing he heard was his Mum's voice:

"Samuel! Wake up! I've made you your favourite!"

Rubbing his eyes, and grateful that he'd just been dreaming and that it was now the school holidays, Sam replied, "Coming, Mum."

Crawling out of bed and slowly making his way downstairs in his pyjamas, his Mum greeted him at the bottom of the stairs with a kiss.

"How is the birthday boy today?" she asked.

"Sleepy," Sam grunted, wiping his cheek and grabbing his breakfast. "I'm excited about my presents. Where is Grandma?" he asked, noticing she wasn't in the lounge like she normally was.

"She's gone for a walk to the lake. She is waiting for you with a special present" his Mum said.

"Oh yeah! Grandma always gives the best presents! I'll go there straight after this!" Sam was so excited and impatient that he started wolfing down his food.

"Slow down, Samuel—it won't run away!" his Mum smiled. Sam took no notice and had soon finished his breakfast, ran upstairs to get changed and was on his way out of the door.

"Bye Mum! I'll be back!"

"Bye. Your other presents will be waiting for you!"

So Sam ran towards the lake as fast as he could go, holding his stomach with his breakfast still inside him. When he arrived at the lake, Sam saw his Grandma from behind. She was standing with her arms held behind her back, her old eyes narrowed and looking out across the water.

"Grandma!" Sam panted, reaching her.

"Hello Dearie," she said, turning and hugging him lightly. "My, you're sweaty. Have you run all this way?" Sam smiled politely, scratching his head for his scalp was itching underneath his short blonde hair.

"Mum said you wanted to see me..."

"Yes, that's right. Happy birthday Dearie" she said, presenting Sam with a wrapped gift which had been placed on a nearby rock.

"Thank you Grandma," Sam blurted, hurriedly opening it. "I don't really know what to—" shock was creeping across his face as he realised "it's...a Bible...Grandma are you sure this is for me?" His Grandma smiled.

"Yes."

"But why would I want a Bible? I really don't read much..."

"Sam, this is the greatest gift I could give you. This is far more than just an ordinary book."

"But Grandma, I'm not really sure if I even believe in God..."

"Look here, Sam, a little faith goes a long way. Turn to the page with the bookmark in, read the highlighted part and do what it says. Trust me." So Sam opened the book to the right section and prepared to read.

"Are you serious?" he asked. His Grandma nodded.

"This is a little embarrassing, but I will do it for you Grandma." Sam walked away a short distance for privacy.

"I'll be right here. Just take your time Dearie," Grandma said. Sam looked down at the lake, and paused when he saw a reflection of himself about to read the Bible. That was something he had never seen before! He took a deep breath, rolled his eyes and read the verse. It was Jeremiah chapter 33 verse 3, which said, "Pray to me and I will answer you. I will tell you important secrets you have never heard before."

Sam found himself talking aloud in response:

"God, if you are real, please prove yourself to me so I can know this book isn't a lame present. If you're not real I know you'll say nothing, which is fine, but my

Grandma won't be very happy..."

Sam was startled by a clattering noise from behind him. He turned to find a sword on the ground and a shield that spun a few times before falling flat. Someone dressed like a Roman soldier was sprawled facedown.

"Are—are you ok?" Sam asked. The person on the floor groaned.

"Hey! Are you hurt?" Sam moved closer to see if he could do anything to help.

The soldier rolled onto his side, checked himself for broken bones and began to crawl towards his things.

"Hello, sorry if I startled you. I'm Maximus," he said, smiling slightly, rubbing his head.

"Sam."

"Yes, I know," Maximus replied. He was a good head shorter than Sam, but more muscular. He had brown hair.

"Do you?"

"Of course. I did have a bit of warning you know."

"About what?" asked Sam, confused.

"That you would be asking for a sign from God," Maximus said. Sam gawped and he couldn't have opened his mouth any wider if he tried.

"Don't look so surprised!" said Maximus. "You had some warning too."

"Warning? What warning?"

"Your Grandma told you to have faith and ask, and here I am!"

"Yes, but you aren't...Him, are you?" Maximus couldn't speak for laughing.

"Who, God? No, definitely not!" His laugh became a calm smile, but his eyes were serious.

"How did you know I'd be asking for a sign from God?" Sam wasn't used to asking quite so many questions. "Anyway why are you dressed as a Roman soldier?"

"I heard you asking God if He was real and I know where we can go to find out. Anyway I am a Roman soldier! Well, at least I will be when I reach the end of the Roman Road" Maximus said, with pride in his voice.

"That's my quest—and when I get there I will stop being a kid in armour and become a man—a legend—a proper Roman soldier!" By now he was waving his sword around in the air, completely lost in the dream.

"Ahem" Sam coughed. Maximus turned. "Well, I wish you the best of luck Maximus," said Sam.

"Thanks, but this is more about skill and bravery than luck. Besides, you're coming with me!"

"What? Don't be ridiculous. What use would I be? Besides, I don't know what the Roman Road is; in fact I don't know where it is, plus — there aren't any Roman soldiers anymore! In any case, it's my birthday and I have presents to unwrap..."

"Exactly!"

"What?"

"You're getting older now, so there's no time to lose. We won't be boys forever. Soldiers like us must train hard for when we become men! I know where the Roman Road is, and you are coming with me!"

"Ok, so you're keen for me to come, but you still haven't said why. I think I believe in God after all this but I'm still not sure what Roman soldiers have to do with anything nowadays, or why you referred to me as a soldier!" Sam was getting his excuses in but he realised he was running out of them.

"You ask a lot of questions Sam! You have a quest to start and so do I. I think I'm here to help you reach the end of the Roman Road, where I will become a soldier and where you will too, though why you don't have any armour I'll never know. That book your Grandma gave you..."

"You mean the Bible?"

"Yes! It will be very useful. In fact I don't think we can make this journey without it."

"Really?" asked Sam.

"Oh yes," Maximus replied. "It will help us in times of trouble and guide us."

"Ok...I think I'm beginning to understand...but where is the Roman Road anyway, and why do we need to walk on it?"

"Oh, it's not far," Maximus said, twiddling his sword. "I've heard if people go far enough on it they find some special armour, and some say they even meet God! But you don't want to keep your Grandma waiting any longer do you?"

"Ah, yes. I wonder what she will make of all this."

Grandma was happy to see Sam again. "Oh hello Dearie. Did you speak with God?"

"Err, yes."

"And what did He say?"

"Well, err, not much but I do have a new friend. Grandma, this is Maximus," he said, introducing him.

"Pleased to meet you, young man," she said. "My, what fine armour you are wearing."

"Thanks," said Maximus. "I will be a real soldier soon."

"Of course you will" Grandma smiled. "Right then boys, I expect you've got a mission to start, a journey to take?"

"Yes, Grandma," Sam replied, "but—"

"Wonderful," she cut him off. "I've made you some birthday cake. Be sure to share it with Maximus. Do Roman soldiers eat cake, Maximus?"

"We eat anything!" he grinned.

"Lovely. Now, Samuel, before you go, here is my final gift to you." She reached into her pocket and pulled out a wooden cross on a thread. "This is more than a fashion symbol," she said, putting it around his neck. "Keep it to remind you that God is listening every time we pray, and if you listen He will talk to you!"

"Thanks, Grandma, but—"

"My you look wonderful with that on. I have highlighted the first few verses in your Bible to start you off but you must learn to listen to God for the rest. Right, it's time to say goodbye to Mum. Run along, boys, and enjoy the adventure!

Remember a little faith goes a long way!"

Soon Sam and Maximus were at Sam's house. His Mum was surprised to hear about the upcoming adventure and a little dubious but she liked the cross, was taken by Maximus's lively spirit and trusted in Grandma enough to let them go. Sam loaded his backpack with his birthday gifts plus a few other things—sleeping bag, small tent and other camping essentials, and they were off.

On the way to the Roman Road, with Maximus leading the way, the boys came across Andrew and Nash, the two bullies who Sam had dreamt about. Sam froze upon seeing them, thinking back to his dream.

"Look who it is, Nash," said Andrew, the taller one.

"I know Andrew, it's Sam the loser! What's that you're wearing?" Nash asked, fingering Sam's cross. "And who's your friend? He sure looks like a weirdo!"

"Must be one of his relatives," added Andrew.

"Sam, who are these guys? Want me to sort 'em out for you?" offered Maximus.

"They're not worth it," said Sam, backing off from them.

"Oh really? Then why are you so scared?" Nash taunted. "What's that you've got there?" He asked, touching the wrapped cake that Sam was clutching. Sam pulled away. Maximus had seen enough.

"Lay off him! That's his birthday cake!" he screamed, holding his sword in front of his face.

"Oh yeah? Well here's a birthday bump for you!" Andrew shouted, pushing Sam over. As he fell onto his back his cake was crushed in his hands. The bullies quickly fled as Maximus was whacking Andrew on the bum with the flat of his sword before Sam had even hit the ground. He chased them quite a distance before Sam had got up. As he stood he heard one of them squealing,

"We'll be watching you, Bible boy!" When Maximus was satisfied that they'd had enough he went back to check on Sam.

"Who were those two, Sam?" he asked, sheathing his sword.

"Andrew and Nash, two guys from school." They started walking again.

"Do they always treat you like this?" Maximus asked.

"Yeah, I guess" Sam admitted.

"Then why don't you stand up to them?"

"There's two of them and one of me, and I guess I just don't like to fight," said Sam.

"Well, Sam, we just may make a soldier of you yet," Maximus grinned.

"I don't know about that, but I'll be glad when they leave me alone. Maybe me being a soldier will stop them. Thanks for your help."

"Don't mention it," said Maximus. "We're on this journey together." He pushed back some long overgrown branches which they had been approaching. "Look, here begins our quest on the Roman Road! Now where is that cake?" he asked, both of them stepping beyond the branches.

"It's here, but it got a bit squashed back there..." Sam looked down in regret,

producing the cake.

"No problem, it's the taste that counts," said Maximus.

"You're right, you Roman soldiers will eat anything!" Sam joked.

So it was that our two friends found the Roman Road. They didn't know what they would encounter on it or how long their journey would take, but Sam had learned that when we talk to God He answers, and that a little faith can go a long way. To find out how far Sam's little faith would take him there was only one way to go—forwards.

To think about:

Do you ever pray? If so, what do you say?

Do you think God ever speaks to you? If not, do you think He could?

Have you ever asked God to speak to you when you read the Bible?

CHAPTER II

A Break in Communication

Sam and Maximus were walking along the Roman Road. Maximus was casually chopping away at the tall grass with his sword, Sam was talking, and they were walking really slowly.

"There's still something I don't understand," said Sam.

"What's that?" Maximus said, distracted.

"My Grandma seemed to know that this day was coming, and she didn't seem surprised when you arrived—and a Roman soldier of all people!"

"Nope," said Maximus, still chopping away haphazardly at the grass.

"But why wasn't she freaked out?" Sam asked.

Maximus stopped. "Look Sam, I think God wants us to help each other. We both need to travel the Roman Road and your Grandma knows that your Bible will help. I have no doubt that your Grandma has been praying for a time like this for a while now."

Sam also stopped. "Oh...Uh-huh. And are you—"

"Yes?"

"Are you...an angel?"

Maximus laughed hard, so hard in fact that he started rolling around on the floor.

"Haha! Sam that's a good one. You are a scream!"

Sam's annoyance went unseen as Maximus stood up.

"No, I am not," he said. "I'm a Roman soldier in training. I'm here to help you though."

"And how are you going to do that?" Sam asked, slightly disbelieving.

"Well, all I know is that we must travel this road together, until we reach the end.

It will be good training for me and I think you will find whatever it is God wants you to find."

"I don't quite get what that could be but maybe it will make sense later," said Sam. "My Grandma told me to read a bit of the Bible each day for guidance, but how will we need guiding? Surely we just keep walking? I mean everyone knows that Roman Roads are straight, right?"

"Yes, but reading is your task," said Maximus. "I'm the soldier, you're the reader. I know it doesn't seem fair, but there you go. The Bible will help you make good decisions I think, and will help you learn."

"Want to swap this for your sword?" Sam said, waving his Bible around. He imagined how cool it would be to have a sword in his hand instead. He could teach Andrew and Nash a lesson or two if he had one of those!

"No way! " said Maximus. "It's your task. There isn't much need for soldiers to read, but why don't you open it and take a look? We should probably rest for a while anyway." So the boys took a rest, Maximus laying down against a tree and eating an apple from it, and Sam sat upon a large rock, his head propped up by his left hand as he reluctantly flicked through the Bible with his right.

"How do I know where to start? It's so big!" Sam despaired.

"How should I know? " Maximus protested. "Wake me up when you find out though." He slouched to the ground, tossed his apple away and began to drift off to sleep. Sam flicked though the pages, homed in on the contents section, running his finger along the titles of the books within the Bible. Eventually he stopped when

he got to the book of Romans, which reminded him of the Roman Road. When he turned to it he found the first verse to be highlighted by his Grandma. Bingo! It was Romans chapter 3 verse 10, which read:

"There is no one who always does what is right, not even one."

Sam thought about it for a bit, by which time Maximus was snoring. Suddenly Sam jumped down from the rock and shook him awake.

3:10?

"Wh-wh—but I don't want to feed the bears," Maximus protested.

"Maximus, wake up! I think I've got it! It's something to do with doing right" said Sam.

"Doing right? asked Maximus.

"Yeah, the Bible said there is no one who always does right." Maximus rubbed his eyes and sat up.

"Ok, well I suppose that's true, but isn't that obvious? I mean, no one can do the right thing all the time, can they?"

"I guess," said Sam. Both of them looked puzzled. Stumped by what to do, and sure that he had read the right part, Sam took out his mobile phone and decided to phone his Grandma. She told them that God was 'righteous' which means He always does right, and we don't always do what is right because we are not like him. Maximus was amazed by the mobile phone as he had never seen one.

"So there is no one like God," said Sam as they started walking again, looking down and holding the cross around his neck. "I guess my Grandma is the closest thing to God that I know, so if she's not like him I can believe that no one is." Maximus murmured in agreement but his thoughts were focused on admiring the phone to take much notice. Though the travellers couldn't see them, two pairs of

eyes were watching them closely from some nearby bushes.

Up ahead of them they heard a noise like something falling into the undergrowth.

"Wait here, Sam," whispered Maximus, quietly drawing his sword. "I'll go and investigate."

"Ok, but be careful, Max," said Sam.

"Max? I like that," Maximus said quietly, poised with his sword out and

stalking into the bushes. Partly to conceal himself in case there was something up ahead, and partly because he was tired, Sam crouched down onto bended knees, and pulled his phone out to check the time. Sam heard footsteps approaching from the direction Maximus went in, and he looked up in horror to see Andrew and Nash, the two bullies, almost on top of him.

"Shout for help and we'll deck you," said Nash.

"What do you want?" asked Sam, intimidated. He rose to his feet but was still a good deal shorter than the others.

"That'll do nicely," said Nash, making a grab for Sam's phone, which spun Sam around so that his back was facing the direction Maximus went. He resisted and clung onto his phone with all his might, but was pushed to the floor. Andrew took his phone and started waving it in front of his face, so Sam tried to fight back and soon found himself on the floor again. In desperate frustration he remembered his Grandma saying that God listens to our prayers.

Still lying flat on his back, he closed his eyes and shot up a quick prayer to God. That was the only thing he could think to do. Time seemed to freeze before he heard terror-filled screams from both of them.

As he opened his eyes, Sam saw them turn tail and run as fast as they could, dropping his phone in the process. It broke. Sam began to stand and turned to find Maximus arriving on the scene.

"Oi! You two leave him alone!" he yelled, waving his sword in defiance. "What happened Sam? What did they want this time?" asked Maximus. Sam, dusting himself down, replied:

"They tried to take my phone. It's broken!"

"What?" asked a shocked Maximus.

"They dropped it when they ran."

"Oh no! At least you've still got it though. Can it be mended?"

"We'll see," said Sam. "I'm glad you came back when you did. I think they are scared of you! So what did you see over there?"

"Nothing. They probably made a noise to draw us apart so they could come out."

"Wow, you know your army tactics!" said Sam, impressed.

"Not well enough if that was anything to go by, but they won't catch me out again," Maximus promised, putting his sword away. "Bullies tend to work in groups because they are cowards. By the way I liked it when you called me Max."

"No problem, Max," said Sam, smiling. They walked on for a while before Sam spoke:

"Max, I think I've learned something."

"Watch out for bullies who want to steal your phone?" Max offered.

"That wasn't quite what I was thinking but it's good advice. I was thinking about there being no one righteous but God."

"Oh. Keep talking," said Max. He was eating the leftovers of Sam's birthday cake.

"Those guys are a great example that people often don't live as God probably wants them to."

"Wow Sam, you're deep," said Max, causing Sam to laugh.

"Haha, no but really, if no one is righteous but God, what can we do?"

"What do you mean?" said Max. Or at least that's what Sam thought he had said, but it was hard to tell because his mouth was so full of cake.

"I mean is there a way we can become like God?" Sam said. "I know some people are kind and do good things for others but if the Bible says that only God is righteous does that mean we are all letting Him down, and He is unhappy with us?"

"Probably," said Max. "But what can we do about that?".

"My Grandma sometimes says that God changed her," said Sam. "I don't really know how He did this though, but I know that she follows Him now so He must have done something good in her life."

"Maybe we'll find out more as we keep walking on the road," Max said hopefully.

"Maybe," Sam sighed. "I just wish I could ring her and ask her for guidance".

"Look, Sam, we've got each other. I've got my sword to protect us and you've got that book in your hand to guide us. If I were you I'd get reading it—and praying," said Max.

Sam looked up and smiled. "You're speaking like my Grandma, Max!"

"Err...sorry?" Max tried, unsure whether it was a good thing or a bad thing.

"No, don't be!" Sam protested. "If I can't ring her now I need the kind of advice that she would normally give for a journey like this."

"No problem, Dearie," Max joked, doing an old lady voice.

"Oi!" Sam yelled.

"Eat your greens, Samuel."

"Max!"

"A little faith goes a long way! Read your Bible..."

"Right that's it soldier boy!"

Sam dived down and hooked Max's legs, taking him to the ground with him, weapons, cake and all. They rolled around locked in a play fight, laughing hysterically amidst Max's impersonations of Sam's Grandma and random sounds of laughter. Anyone nearby would've wondered what was going on, but these were two young guys on a quest from God, not understanding the point of it yet but having the time of their lives all the same.

To think about:

If God is righteous and we are not, can we please him by ourselves? (Romans 8:8)

Do you think that God could change you to live a way that pleases him?

Are you or any of your friends struggling with bullying? What can you do to make this situation better? Why not ask God to help.

CHAPTER III

Down Under

Sam and Max were resting by a stream. Sam was filling up his water bottle and Max was knelt down splashing water on his face.

"So why a soldier, Max? What's the appeal for you?" asked Sam.

"Huh?" Max spluttered whilst washing.

"Why do you want to be a soldier?"

"Roman soldiers have to be tough," said Max. "They win great battles and it's the most exciting way of sharing in the glory of Rome."

"I see. Well, the Roman empire sure was glorious."

"What do you mean, was?" Max looked at Sam annoyed.

"Well, I studied the Roman empire in history class recently. I read all about how great it was—the many conquests, how it expanded, how it rose, and—" Sam paused, "and how it fell."

Max was quick to respond. "Look Sam, I don't care what your history teacher said. When we've finished this quest I'm going straight to Rome to share in the glory of the mightiest empire ever!"

"Ok, Max, sorry," finished Sam. A lengthy silence followed as Max finished washing and Sam sat looking back at the road.

"Should we move on?" he asked.

"I'm right behind you, Sam," said Max as they rose and set off again. After a while Sam spoke:

"Another thing I learned in history class..." Max held his breath "...was that Roman Roads were built on major trade routes to make travelling easier for merchants and soldiers."

"Very true," said Max.

"So I'm just wondering why this road was pretty much hidden. I mean I'd never heard of it or seen it before even though it was close to my house, and we haven't seen anyone on it yet apart from Andrew and Nash."

"Sam, just because you haven't seen many people on the Road doesn't mean it isn't worth journeying on."

"Fair enough. Max, look! I see some people!" Sam pointed ahead where, in the distance, they saw two figures emerging at the top of the hill they were headed towards. "Let's try and catch up to them." Sam started to run with Max in pursuit, and Max was soon level pegging despite the weight of his armour. As they gained on the travellers they realised before long that they were walking towards them. As they drew close one of the strangers spoke:

"Hello there," said one of them, a thin lady with blonde shoulder-length hair. The boys stopped.

"Hi," said Sam, red-faced with effort.

"What's your rush?"said the other person, a tall man with a ginger goatee beard and a red rucksack.

"We hadn't really seen anyone on this road yet so we got excited when we saw you," said Sam. The lady smiled, saying:

"Thanks. I'm Danielle and this is my husband, Kieran."

"Hi guys," he said. Both boys smiled at him. They looked at Max, who said hello. The four of them got chatting and before long they were sharing lunch together; a simple meal of Danielle and Kieran's sandwiches with Sam's water and crisps.

"So where are you boys heading?" asked Danielle.

"To the end of the road" said Sam. The adults seemed taken aback by his response.

Max, curious, asked "How about you?"

"We're going back to the beginning. We couldn't get past the next bit" said the lady.

"Why not?" asked Sam, his ever-inquisitive mind rather curious. "What's up there?" he motioned with a nod to the brow of the hill where he'd first spotted them.

"It's tough guys, and it didn't make sense to us!" said Kieran.

"It's nothing to be afraid of," said Danielle, "but we hope for your sake that you fare better than us."

"Why don't you come with us and try again?" asked Sam optimistically. The couple looked at each other.

"No point," said Kieran, defeated. "We haven't done anything wrong."

Soon they were parting ways, Sam and Max continuing on and the others heading back.

"Good luck, boys, you'll need it," shouted Danielle.

"I'm not sure I believe in luck," Sam thought aloud as they walked. "Not when God's involved."

"Hmm-mm," agreed Max. They kept walking, wondering what could be ahead. As they reached the top of the hill they saw a forest up ahead of them. It was thick, with trees as far as the eye could see. The road ran right into the heart of it.

"I wonder if Robin Hood is at home," Sam joked, as they got closer to it.

"Robin who?" asked a puzzled Max.

"Never mind."

They entered the forest. The trees were tall, arching overhead, and the road, though still visible, was covered with fallen branches. The wind up ahead could not be felt because of the trees, and they were so dense that it was becoming warm.

"What's that?" blurted Max, his hand on the hilt of his sword. They paused. Up ahead was the tallest tree either of them had ever seen. It was so big that their necks craned and they couldn't see the top, and so wide that it covered the entirety of the

road. There was no way around it and climbing was definitely not an option.

"This must be what Danielle and Kieran were talking about," said Sam, searching for a way through. "I've never seen anything so huge." He noticed '3:23' etched into the bark just above his head. "What do you think that means?" he asked.

"Dunno. Maybe that's how many years the tree has been here for?" tried Max.

"Mmm..." wondered Sam.

"Try asking God?" Max suggested.

"Yes! You may be onto something there. I haven't read the Bible yet today," said Sam excitedly. He rummaged in his bag, pulled the Bible out and opened it up to the next highlighted verse.

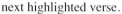

"Max! You won't believe this. It's Romans chapter 3 verse 23! My Grandma highlighted this so we are on the right track!"

"Max rushed to Sam's side and together he and Sam read it aloud: "All have sinned and are not good enough for God's glory.""

"What do you think it means Sam?"

"Not sure." He sat down to think. Max did his thinking by hacking at nearby branches with his sword. Sam prayed. "Please God, show us what we need to see. Show us the way." A moment later, Sam's vacant look slowly turned to one of realisation.

"Max! I think I'm getting it!" Max looked at him, still hacking away.

"You know what sin means?" Sam pressed on.

"Isn't that when you've done something wrong?"

"Yes. Kieran said he and Danielle have done nothing wrong but it says here that all have sinned. And how would you define glory? You used that word to talk about Rome earlier."

"Glory," said Max, waving his sword around and looking down the shaft towards the end. "Glory is success, might; something glorious is truly amazing and, like Rome, everyone should admire and respect it."

"Right," said Sam, "and God is so glorious that no one is like Him. We learned before that He is the only one who is righteous."

"Yes," said Max, as Sam's train of thought continued.

"And because everyone has done wrong, no one is good enough for God's glory, meaning no one can match up to it."

"Makes sense," Max contributed.

"So, if we can't get up to God's glory—

"—we should get down!" Max blurted.

"What?"

"I've seen it in the empire. When people are showing respect or awe for Caesar, they bow down before him."

"So you're saying we should bow down before God?" asked Sam.

"Yeah, I guess," said Max. So the two friends slowly got down on their knees, Sam following Max's example. They knelt down, their heads low, saying nothing. It didn't take long for at least one of them to feel rather foolish.

"Now what?" said Sam.

"Now we—err...Sam, look at that!" Max jumped up, spotting something his hacking had uncovered. "A hole in the ground! I bet this goes under the tree. We definitely need to go down!" Both of them hurriedly scraped away the last of the camouflage.

"I'll go first Sam," said Max.

"But-"

"—I'm the smallest. I'll go check it's safe." Before Sam could get another word out, Max had gone. Sam looked around.

"Please God, keep him safe," he prayed. A few minutes later, he heard muffled shouts from the other side of the tree.

Sam couldn't make out the words but followed Max nonetheless. The hole was big enough but very dark, and thankfully he could hear Max's voice now and again. Sam followed his shouts as the tunnel steadily became lighter, and after what felt like half an hour Sam's soil-covered head popped up on the other side of the tree.

"Thank you," he said.

"Wow, Sam!" laughed Max. "Your head is sticking out of the tree!" Sam smiled, relieved to be in the daylight again.

"Wasn't yours?"

"No! I came out of this hole!" Max pointed to a hole in the ground near his feet.

"Whoa, it's like London Underground in here," quipped Sam, climbing out of the hole and back onto the road.

"What's London Underground?" asked Max. Sam hadn't thought that Roman soldiers probably weren't familiar with such things so he began to tell Max about Covent Garden, Piccadilly Circus and all the intricate series of tunnels that the London trains run along. They were dusting themselves down and having a drink of water, looking out into the forest that remained before them, when they heard a yell from somewhere behind them.

"What was that?" stopped Sam.

"It came from down here. Someone is in the tunnel!" said Max.

"Who's down there?" called Sam, in a press-up position next to the hole Max had emerged from. Max, suspicious, peered into the hole in the tree where Sam had been.

"Help! Samuel, Roman boy—anyone please help!" came a desperate shout.

"I recognise that voice," said Sam to Max. "It's Andrew."

"The ratbag who broke your phone?" said Max.

"Yeah."

"How ironic that the guy who picks on you now wants our help!"

"Yes, but we should really help them," said Sam.

Sam shouted back, "What's wrong?"

"It's Andrew and Nash," came the reply. "We're stuck down here!"

"We're coming, hold on! Sam was almost on his way down, and just then he remembered his torch, kicking himself for not using it the first time. "You'll like this, Max," he said, showing him the light.

"Wow! Your stick makes light!"

"Yeah, and I'll tell you about it when I come back."

"When you come back? Sam, I don't like this. Those guys have been nothing but mean to you. What if they hurt you down there?"

"It's a chance I need to take for their sake. And I need to borrow your belt please."

"For what?" asked Max, shocked again.

"To pull them up!"

"Ok, ok," said Max, reluctantly passing it over. "Constance and I are right here if you need us" he said, kissing his sword.

"Constance!" laughed Sam, turning towards the tree hole with the torch and belt.

"Well I've got to call her something..." Max's voice tailed off as Sam crawled in, shuffling on his front towards the voices below.

"Where are you guys?" he asked, his torch light revealing the many intersections of the tunnel and just how fortunate he and Max had been to make it through the first time. Sam followed the cries for help and a few minutes later found both Andrew and Nash. Nash had his foot caught on something but Andrew was too big to turn and release him. Sam wriggled past them both, causing much pain and discomfort to all three of them. He found the offending item to be a root wrapped around Nash's

foot, which he prized apart by wrapping the belt around it and tugging with all his might. Nash's foot was free. Sam managed to turn by doing a very awkward roly poly and followed the others towards Max, who was now shouting to them so that they knew where he was. Andrew and Nash emerged first through the hole Max had used earlier. He was waiting there with sword drawn and shield ready. Andrew and Nash, who were much bigger than Max, crawled out on all fours and, exhausted, showed no signs of getting up anytime soon.

"Where is Sam?" challenged Max, aggressively, just as Sam's head emerged.

"Right here, Max," he replied.

"Thanks," muttered Andrew. "We were really stuck back there. We owe you one."

"Don't say that!" snapped Nash. "We owe them nothing."

"You owe him a phone that works," asserted Max, "not to mention gratitude for saving you down there!"

"Shut up, Rome-eo," snapped Nash.

"Lay off him, Nash, they saved us," Andrew retorted. Nash went quiet, defeated and embarrassed.

"Why are you following us?" said Sam.

"Don't tell him," said Nash. Andrew didn't.

"Alright then," said Max, pointing with his sword. "You two stop following us and we'll say no more about it. Come on, Sam, let's get going." Sam looked back at Andrew and Nash. They exchanged glances with him but no one said anything. Sam attempted his best smile, aimed it at Andrew and turned to walk with Max, returning his belt to him.

"So tell me about your stick that makes light," said Max.

"It's called a torch, and the light comes on when you press the button."

"Ah." Max seemed satisfied with this knowledge and was enjoying playing with it.

"Now tell me more about Constance," Sam grinned. The two friends continued through the forest unaware of what lay ahead but hopeful that Andrew and Nash had been left behind. Their faith in God had grown, and they had learned that all have done wrong and are not good enough for God's glory. With Sam in search of their next challenge, and Max in search of their next meal, they carried on into the forest. More adventures awaited them on the Roman Road...

To think about:

Just as Danielle and Kieran believed, do you think it is possible to live a life without doing anything wrong?

What do you do when you are tempted to do something you know to be wrong?

Max and Sam bowed down to God, realising they needed His help. Are there things in your life where you would appreciate God's help? What are you going to do about it?

CHAPTER IV

A Puzzling Sign

Sam woke up to the smell of food. He and Max had left the tunnel behind them and followed the road further into the forest where they had spent the night halfway up a tree. It was sturdy and they had found alcoves to sleep in where the branches met. Max's fit him comfortably but Sam had to struggle to fit into his. He had slept one half of the night curled up in a ball and the other half with his feet slightly elevated, which strained his neck. Still, it was safer than sleeping on the ground. As Sam rose, rubbing his neck and trying to regain some feeling in his legs, he looked down to see Max sitting on the ground. He was holding his sword over a little fire, humming to himself. Smelling bread, Sam climbed down as nimbly as he could (which wasn't very nimble at all) and plopped to the ground. Max turned.

"Morning," he said. "Sleep well?"

Sam groaned the kind of groan that suggested he didn't. Rubbing his eyes, now he noticed that Max had several slices of bread on his sword. He was making toast.

"Woah, remind me never to talk to you first thing in the morning," he grinned. Sam complained that he hadn't slept at all well and Max, who had been rather comfortable, failed to see his point of view.

"I don't want any toast anyway!" Sam blurted after a while, so Max sat there eating it completely dry. All was absolutely silent and the only sound that could be heard was Max crunching away. Sam opened up his Bible and read Romans 6:23. It was the last verse highlighted by his Grandma. He read: "When people sin, they earn what sin pays—death".

"Max?" Sam asked. All he heard was the laboured munching of dry toast.

"Mmm? You're talking to me now are you?"

"Yes," said Sam. Fear-stricken at the 'D' word he promptly said sorry to Max for being grumpy before producing a jar of peanut butter from his bag. Max, bewildered, asked what it was.

"Peanut butter. You spread it on your toast. It'll rock your world." Sam gave him a plastic knife for spreading.

"Thanks!" said Max, excited after smelling it and beginning to slap it on the remainder of his toast. "Why the sudden apology and kindness?"

"Mind if I borrow Constance?" asked Sam, referring to Max's sword.

"No, but be careful with her." Sam put the last few slices of their bread on Max's sword and began to make his own toast as he said, "I just read the next Bible passage."

"What did it say?" asked Max, mid-chew.

"It said that when people sin they earn what sin pays—death."

"You mean death is a punishment for what we do wrong?" Max asked.

"That's what it said." Both paused. Max stopped chewing.

"Wow, that's heavy," said Max. "When I become a proper Roman soldier I will get paid. We sometimes call it 'wages', but the wages of being a soldier are not death! Are you sure you've read that right?"

"Yes," Sam replied. "Max I'm sorry for being an idiot this morning. I was angry because you had slept well and I hadn't. I had no right to take it out on you."

"Thanks," said Max, chewing again. "I know that was hard for you. Will there always be peanut butter when you've done something wrong?" Sam laughed a faint laugh, rotating his toast.

"I'm worried," he said, staring into the fire. "If all have sinned and aren't good enough for God's glory, and if death is a punishment for sin, what's going to happen to us? Where does this road lead to?" Max was keen to reassure him:

"Look, I don't know the answers to those questions but your Grandma wouldn't have packed you off on this adventure if there would be death at the end," Max assured, half-hearted.

"I guess you're right," said Sam. He also had peanut butter on his toast. Max watched him spread it, hoping he would save some for later. Once Sam had finished his toast and they'd both had a drink (berry juice with a little water) they followed the road again. It was almost midday. The road continued through the forest, which seemed to Sam as though it would never end. Two hours later however they noted

how the trees seemed thinner and were more spread out. The forest was coming to an end and the two friends kept walking, cautious of what may lie ahead and worried about the Bible passage. Sam walked in front, his head down, deep in thought. Max was a few yards behind, swapping his shield arm regularly due to the weight. He was looking ahead, and called out as he saw the forest disappearing: "I think I see something!"

The road was beginning to incline a little as Sam looked up, and there was in the distance what looked to be a telegraph pole. As they drew nearer they noticed it appeared to be a large signpost, and they began to make out the figure of a person standing below it, hands on hips. The man was staring up at the sign which stood roughly three metres high. Sam and Max approached and noticed the sign pointing in two opposite directions. The word 'GIFT' was pointing ahead of them and the word 'WAGES' back towards the forest.

"Hello?" offered Sam. The man didn't seem to notice them. On closer inspection Max saw "6:23" written on the pole.

Sam tried again.

"Err, hello? Mister?" The man turned.

"Eh? What's that? Hello, young sirs. Did you say something just now?"

"Yes," replied Sam, feeling awkward.

"Then pardon me. I thought I heard something but was in my own world."

"No problem," said Sam. "What does the sign mean?"

The man was of average height with dark, greying hair. He had bushy eyebrows and glasses. Sam would have put him in his late forties.

"Ah, another inquisitive mind. Good. Many folks would probably just walk on with the road being as straight as this, but it's good to ask questions." They looked at him intently, hopeful for answers.

"To be honest boys I'm not too sure what it means." Sam tried to hide his disappointment. Max, who was always wary of strangers and hadn't said anything yet, spoke up:

"I think you should read your Bible, Sam."

"But I've read it already today and I don't really like what it says, unless my Grandma highlighted the wrong bit."

"Romans 6:23?" asked Max.

"How did you know?" a shocked Sam replied.

"Because it's written on the post."

"So it is," Sam smiled, embarrassed. He pulled his Bible out and read the verse aloud, only this time he noticed there was a second part to it. Earlier he was unable to read past 'death', but now it read "When people sin, they earn what sin pays—death. But God gives us a free gift—life for ever in Christ Jesus our Lord."

"That's more like it!" said Max.

"I knew there had to be another piece to the jigsaw!" said Sam.

"Eternal life!" Max smiled. Sam hooked his arm around Max's and tried to make him dance. Both boys laughed—Sam with relief at the verse and Max at Sam's state of excitement. Thankfully for Max he had never seen Sam on a sugar high, but this is the kind of excitement we are talking about. As Sam was dancing and Max was being spun around, Max remembered the stranger and noticed that he was looking downcast. Seeing the man's face he asked:

"Are you ok, sir?" His serious tone made Sam stop dancing.

"Not really," the man replied. His gaze returned to the sign.

"What's the matter?" Sam asked. "We just read that the gift is eternal life!" The

man kept staring. Sam didn't think he was going to reply. He re-read the verse. Max's eyes flicked between the two of them, aware of the awkward silence but unaware how to break it. Eventually the man turned to Sam.

"It's Jesus," he said. Sam and Max looked at each other.

"What about him?" Sam asked.

"People say so much about him. I've heard so many different things I just don't know what to believe." He sank to the floor. Max asked Sam for a drink as they sat down too. It was a time of mixed feelings. The boys were happy to have left the forest behind, and though initially confused by the sign and scared of where the road may lead, they were thrilled to read about the prospect of eternal life. Then they heard the man nearby feeling upset by what they thought was good news.

"That cross around your neck," he said to Sam. "Why do you wear it? What does it mean?"

"My Grandma gave it to me. She told me that God listens when I pray," Sam said with a glint of pride.

"You a Christian then?" the man asked.

"I dunno," Sam replied, "but God's been doing stuff in my life recently..." Sam sat a little closer to him and began sharing with him about their adventure so far. Max joined in. It turned out that the man was called Tony. He had been an accountant all his life before joining the Roman Road.

"Isn't everyone in England born a Christian?" Sam asked as they all shared their food and drink with each other.

"People think that but there are people of all sorts of faiths in England, and all over the world. People can be brought up a certain way but in the end we are all free to choose what we believe," Tony said. "Someone told me once that even going to church doesn't make you a Christian."

He had a good look at the Bible and lent Sam his mobile phone so that he could ring home. Sam's Mum was sorry to hear about his broken phone and was keen to know that they were eating enough. When Grandma spoke Max, fascinated by the technology though not aware of its limits, asked her if she could send some cake down the phone. Grandma assured him he could have some next time they met.

The sun was beginning to drop as they returned the phone to Tony. Max was keen to keep going and rose to his feet. Sam, as determined as before to press on, did the same. Tony, despite encouragements to go with them, decided to wait at the sign and think some more. So the boys said farewell to their new friend, taking to the road again.

They were excited about the prospect of eternal life and wondered what Jesus had to do with it and wondered which way Tony would go and if they would see him again. They walked in silence, thinking about these things, hoping and believing that they were going the right way. Glancing back Sam noticed two figures following them at a distance. They looked familiar which made his stomach wrench, but he looked down at the wooden cross around his neck and for some reason only that seemed to matter.

To think about:

Do you know any Christians? If so, how does following Jesus make a difference in their lives? Does eternal life sound like something you would like?

Tony had some big questions which were making it hard for him to keep walking on the Roman Road. Do you have any big questions about life or faith? Why not talk to a Christian you know about them, such as a minister or youth leader? Why not talk to God?

CHAPTER V

Some Surprises

It was raining. No, that's not true—it was bucketing down. For Sam and Max, two adventurers following a very straight Roman Road for miles out in the open, it was a very miserable time indeed. Sam, being the tallest, was carrying Max's shield flat above their heads as a makeshift umbrella. The two friends were so water-logged that their clothes were sticking to them, and the grey-black clouds above them showed no signs of disappearing.

"This is hopeless," sniffled Max.

"I have an idea," Sam replied, having to shout above the sound of heavy water droplets crashing all around them. "I don't know why I didn't think of it before." He promptly produced his tent, and after a frantic few minutes of teamwork it was up and they were inside. The floor was damp as there was no dry ground to pitch the tent on, and the boys had been in such a rush to erect it that they didn't even think about putting the pegs in—not that they would have been much use on the old concrete of the road. Thankfully the rain kept the tent in position well enough. Sam began to change into his only other clothes in order to try and avoid catching a cold. Now Roman soldiers rarely take their armour off; in fact Max would sleep in his,

so he took his chances. Sam shone his torch on the wall of the tent, making animal faces with his hands. Max called it his 'light stick'. Sam made a dog, a squirrel and even a mosquito shape. Max was convinced that he could make a bear but to Sam it looked more like a cat.

The rain continued as they decided that, with them likely to be there for a while, they would sit down. It was still damp but they made the best of it. Sam told Max about how he liked to entertain himself when he wasn't stuck inside a wet tent, telling him about his Playstation and all his favourite games. Max, who was normally fascinated by technology, didn't seem to understand why it would be so much fun playing a game from a chair indoors when there was so much fun to be had outside.

"What do you like to do for fun then?" Sam asked.

"I like to paint."

"You paint?" Max looked down and paused, as though embarrassed. "Wow, Max, I never thought of you like that.

What kind of things do you like to paint?" Max then went on a roll—he really opened up and described vividly how he loved nature and the beauty of the world—the sea, the sky, mountains—you name it, Max painted it. This was a new side to him that Sam had never seen. It was a sensitive side, in direct contrast to Max the warrior. Sam loved it.

By now, sleep-deprived since their night in the tree, Sam was tired, and before he knew it he was having a nap. He dreamt that he was asleep on his own bed with two feather pillows and fresh sheets. It was his birthday and his Mum was calling him downstairs for breakfast. When he walked downstairs the kitchen turned into a giant floating Bible, which he followed for miles, and sat on it was a Roman soldier boy throwing paint at him and shouting "5 8! 5 8!" over and over again. Sam

woke up suddenly and realised he had been dreaming. Still groggy, he lifted his head to find Max sitting upright, sucking something.

"I hope you don't mind," he said, "but I'm eating peanut butter. We haven't eaten since we saw Tony and I'm famished."

"No problem," said Sam, slowly rising. "How are we doing for water?"

"Our next drink will be the last of it," replied Max, glumly. "At least it's stopped raining now. Are you ready to get marching again?"

Sam looked outside. The road was drenched but at least it was brightening up. "Yeah, let's go." They packed up their tent and were soon walking again, and now that it wasn't so gloomy all around they could see fields on every side. There were no crops or animals, only mud and grass. The smell of rain was heavy on the air, and the relief of having escaped a lot of it inside the tent soon vanished when ankle-deep puddles reminded them they were at nature's mercy. Sam began to talk to God, asking him that neither of them would catch a cold.

He also prayed for drinking water, and that God would keep his family safe. He found himself thinking that he should read his Bible again, and he reached for it as they walked. Taking it out he felt a sudden sharp jolt in the back of his knees as his legs buckled and the book was wrenched from his grasp. Max spun in response and reached for his sword but was rugby tackled to the ground before he could respond. Sam stayed down sprawled flat on his front, recovering from the attack as he heard the footprints of his attacker hurriedly splashing away from him, and nearby grunts as Max was interlocked in a scuffle. Sam turned his head to see Max and Andrew rolling on the ground. One was on top and then the other was, both scrambling for supremacy. Max was much shorter but was stronger than Andrew had expected. Sam, seizing the initiative, pounced on Andrew and the two of them soon had him pinned down. He was lying on his back looking up at Max, who was

standing above him pointing his sword down at him, gathering his breath. Sam stood nearby clutching Max's shield.

Andrew wasn't going anywhere fast. The surprise attack had failed from his point of view, and Nash was nowhere to be seen.

"What is your problem?" Max fumed.

"It was Nash's idea" Andrew chirped.

"What was?" asked Max.

"Taking the book," he replied.

"The book?" Max went on. "What book? Sam, have you still got your Bible?"

"No, they took it," he admitted, rubbing his legs. "Well, Nash did."

"Look, we didn't mean you any harm," Andrew added. "We only wanted to see what it said."

"Then why didn't you ask?" Max barked. And anyway I thought I warned you not to follow us?" Andrew lay still.

"I don't think he's coming back," said Max, looking around. "Some friend you have there."

"Come on, Max, lay off him. He's obviously not behind this," said Sam, helping Andrew up. They talked for a while and even Max began to relax as time passed. Andrew told that Nash said they should read it because of how it seemed to be helping Sam and Max make decisions.

"Sorry to disappoint you but it's not a magic book of spells or anything like that," said Sam. "But God speaks through it, so you could say it's better than magic!"

"Wow," said Andrew. He fell silent again, now thinking deeply. Eventually he spoke. "I always thought it was possible to speak to God but I never thought He would speak back," he admitted, thoughts whirring through his mind.

"He definitely does," Max asserted.

"And we need it back!" Sam said. Andrew could sense the urgency in his voice.

Max carried on "God is guiding us on our quest. We need that book to understand the next part!" Max kicked at the dirt. Sam looked at Andrew, who grinned and said: "Then let's go and get it!"

"Alright!" said Sam. "Thank you." Max let out a whoop. As Andrew led them to where he thought Nash would be, he said sorry for following them and particularly to Sam for breaking his phone and picking on him at school.

"It makes me feel big to pick on people who are smaller than me," he said, "but when I look at you guys I realise you are happy and you don't need to do anything like that to feel that way."

"Thanks, Andrew, you're right," said Sam, touched by his honesty. "Plus there aren't many people smaller than Max!"

All three of them burst out laughing. Andrew shared some of his water with them. Sam had goose pimples and felt warm inside as though he was making a new friend. They found Nash a little farther along the road. He was sitting on a tree stump, looking at the Bible. He didn't seem happy to see Andrew with Max and Sam.

"What are you doing with those idiots?" he scoffed. Max reached for his sword. Even Sam, remembering his painful fall, wanted to hurt Nash, but Andrew gestured to them both to relax.

"Look, these guys are ok," he said. "I'm learning a lot from them."

"Oh yeah?" asked Nash, unbelievingly. "Do you think they can make sense of this stupid book?"

"We normally do ok," said Sam. "But you've got to ask God to explain it to you."

"What? God? I knew you two were ridiculous but this takes the mick! Wake up and realise there is no God!" And with that he knocked the Bible off his lap and onto the wet ground. Sam was hurt by this but didn't want to let it show. Max beat his sword on his shield. Andrew stooped and picked the Bible up, wiped it on his sleeve and returned it to Sam.

"Sorry guys," he said. "I think you'd better keep going." Sam understood what he meant — that Andrew didn't want to leave his friend even though he was ashamed of his behaviour.

"Ok, Andrew," said Sam. "Thanks." As he and Max began to walk away he excitedly told Max about his dream. "It's 5:8, I'm sure of it! We have to read Romans 5:8!" He thumbed through his now slightly crumpled Bible and said "Please God show us what you want us to see", then he read Romans chapter 5 verse 8 aloud. It

said: "But God shows his great love for us in this way: Christ died for us while we were still sinners."

"What do you think that means?" asked Max.

"Well we read last time that sin leads to death but that Jesus makes eternal life possible..."

"Yes..." said Max, hoping Sam would keep going. He did.

"So I guess this explains how."

"What do you mean?" Max asked. He remembered what they'd learned before now but 5:8 was a little confusing.

"Well, you know that Jesus Christ was killed on a cross?"

"Yes," said Max. "One of Rome's less glorious moments."

"Yeah, well I think this is saying that he did this for our sins. He chose to die for us, and somehow this leads to eternal life even though we all do bad things which make God upset with us."

"Woah Sam, you're good at this Bible reading stuff." Just as he spoke Max's stomach rumbled violently. "I sure hope we find some food before we find eternal life or we may never get there!" Sam laughed, put his Bible back in his bag, and prayed. He thanked God for the road behind, for Max, for Andrew, and for the road ahead. He said sorry for things he had done wrong and prayed that he and Max would find eternal life—and food, on the Roman Road. As their feet walked in puddles reminding them of the rain from earlier, Max caught a glimmer of light amongst the dark clouds above. The Roman Road promised hope, built faith, and Max was convinced that love was on there too.

To think about:

Is it a surprise that Jesus died for us while we were still sinners? Who should get all the credit for forgiving and changing a person?

One great formula for talking to God is to say a 'Teaspoon prayer.' It simply means 'Thank you, sorry, please' and we can remember it from the letters 'T' 'S' and 'P' in 'teaspoon.' Sam's prayer at the end was a teaspoon prayer.

Have you ever said a teaspoon prayer? Why not have a go now. All you have to do is thank God for the things you want to thank him for, say sorry for the things you have done wrong, and then you are ready to say please on behalf of others and yourself.

CHAPTER VI

Chocolate Eggs, an Orange and an Empty Tomb

"Achoo!" Max sneezed. It wasn't his first of the day by any means. He'd caught a cold from his and Sam's adventure in the rain. Sam meanwhile felt completely fine. He was so happy to see a bright sky with no dark clouds in, and so excited about the eternal life that awaited them that he started to skip!

"Whad in da world are you doink?"asked Max through a bunged-up nose. Sam, not usually one for skipping, realised that macho Roman soldiers were probably even less likely to do it.

"Err, I was..."struggling to find an excuse for skipping, Sam persuaded Max to try and forget it had happened, so they kept walking with Sam trying to overcome his embarrassment and Max trying to stifle a laugh. Their mouths were dry and their stomachs were growling, especially Max's because he had the biggest appetite, but they carried on walking.

There was a breeze and it had been raining. Max liked the smell of the rain. There were crops in the fields now along with sheep and cows, with trees dotted to the left and to the right. Seeing all these signs of life made home feel like a very long way away for Sam. What he wouldn't have given right then for a fish finger sandwich! Food would have to wait though. There were more people on this section of the road than Sam and Max had seen so far; people from different parts of the world. On the road was a big '10:9' marked out in different coloured stones. It had been here as long as the road itself for it was part of it, and the handful of people nearby were reacting to it in different ways—reading their Bibles, walking straight past, talking about it or even leaving the road altogether and splitting off in different directions. Sam pulled his Bible out to see for himself. Romans 10:9 said, "If you use

your mouth to say, "Jesus is Lord," and if you believe in your heart that God raised Jesus from the dead, you will be saved." An elderly couple called Rowland and Margaret joined them. They were Christians who had been married for many years, and though they had been through great hardships they said God had given them the strength to overcome them. They were farmers, and as their farm was very close by, the boys accepted their invitation for food.

Max, usually wary of new people, somehow knew that he could trust them. He and Sam helped Rowland chop wood for the fire whilst Margaret prepared the meal. They ate really well and their stomachs were soon satisfied as they enjoyed dish after dish of tasty food. After dinner the boys entertained Rowland and Margaret by acting out their adventures in front of the fire, to enthusiastic applause. When he heard how God had guided them along the road, Rowland asked them if they had read Romans 10:9 yet and what they thought about it.

"I think we understand what it means to call Jesus 'Lord'," said Sam. "It's something to do with saying there is no one like him, and he is the way we can live forever."

"Good, yes," said Rowland. "He knows best and we need to follow him."

"Yeah," said Sam. "How can we get eternal life? Also, isn't he dead? Max said he was crucified by the Romans. If this is true how can he give us eternal life?"

"Good questions, Sam," Rowland smiled. "First, what can you tell me about Easter?"

"I love the chocolate eggs. Yum!" said Sam.

"Chucolad eggs?" said Max, confused, his cold showing no signs of going.

"Yeah, giant eggs made out of chocolate. They are so nice. Mum says I should make them last but I just want to eat as many as I can."

"Ahem," coughed Rowland. He had their attention again. "So we've covered chocolate eggs, but you haven't told me why we celebrate Easter."

"My Grandma always says we should go to church at Easter but we don't tend to" Sam admitted.

Rowland picked up an orange from his fruit bowl. "This isn't chocolate or even an egg, but it will do. The real meaning of Easter..." the boys leaned in, "is that Jesus Christ never did anything wrong. He led a life free of sin, and was killed on a cross as a sacrifice for all our sins—yours, mine, everyone's. Sin takes us away from God and He wants us to be close to Him. He loves us so much that He sent his son Jesus to take the punishment for our sins so we can be close to Him again."

"Wow," exclaimed Max. "Bud whad's thad godda do wid Easder, or dad oraj?"

"Jesus was crucified on a Friday which we call 'Good Friday'. It wasn't good because he died, but what his death achieved is very good news! Those who follow him—like Margaret and I, are called Christians, and though we're not perfect, Jesus gives us the power to keep trying to live like him. He helps us to start again with God by making us new inside. We remember on Easter Sunday, two days after Good Friday, that the tomb Jesus was buried in was found empty! No one could find his body! Easter eggs, or in my example this orange, remind us of the stone covering the tomb that was rolled away to reveal an empty grave. Jesus had risen!"

"So whad happened do iz boday?" asked Max.

"He rose from the grave!" Rowland

exclaimed, getting excited. "He spent time with his followers teaching them and giving them a wonderful gift called the Holy Spirit, and then he went up to heaven, where he waits until it's time for him to come to earth again."

"But how do we receive eternal life?" Sam asked, thinking hard.

"That's the best bit," said Rowland. "All you have to do is say sorry to Jesus for all you have done wrong, ask him to be your friend and decide to follow him. He will do the rest!"

"And da Holy Spirid?" asked Max as he blew his nose.

"The Holy Spirit is another helper like Jesus, who Jesus gives as a free gift to all his friends. He gives us the power to follow Jesus. He's who was given to the disciples before he went to heaven, and he will give him to you if you ask!"

Rowland was on the edge of his chair now, buzzing. Margaret, who had been sat silently all this time, added "We can't make the decision for you boys because everyone has to make it for themselves. As Row said, Romans 10:9 means that Jesus really wants to be your friend and give you a new start—a new life! He is always with you! But it's up to you."

Sam and Max looked at each other. All the talk of new beginnings and having Jesus as a very real friend sounded very exciting.

Rowland looked at them both in a serious way and said one last thing. "Romans 10:9 is real, boys. Those who call Jesus 'Lord' and believe God raised him from the dead will be saved – and receive eternal life!"

"I'm in," beamed Sam. "I want to pray the prayer, join the club or whatever I have to do! Please help me become a Christian."

"Me doo!" jumped Max. He wasn't going to pass up on the best news he had ever heard. He'd forgotten that they hadn't eaten dessert yet but right then it didn't even matter.

"Praise God," said Margaret. "Fantastic news boys," Rowland smiled, "but I must warn you that being a friend of Jesus is not just about a ticket to heaven. It is as much about following him in the here and now as it is about that." The boys nodded. "And not everyone will understand your decision to be a Christian. In fact you may even be given a hard time by people who don't understand it, but God will always give you the strength to stand up for the truth" said Rowland.

Sam gulped. He'd already had a hard time from Andrew and Nash without giving them more ammo to have a go at him, but something within him was telling him that he needed Jesus, and that Jesus was stronger than bullies. "I'm no chicken" he said. "Let's do this."

"Yeah!" grinned Max. "I wand do sdand up for Jesus doo!"

Here is the prayer that Rowland and Margaret prayed with Sam and Max:

"Father God, thank you for making me and for loving me. Thank you for sending your only son Jesus to shed his blood and die for me and to take the punishment for all my sins. I am sorry for all I have ever done wrong. Please forgive me and help me to start again. Lord Jesus, I believe in my heart that God raised you from the dead. Please come into my life, be my closest friend and make me new. Please fill me with your Holy Spirit and help me to follow you. Thank you for saving me and for my new start. In Jesus's name, amen."

After they had all finished praying, everyone opened their eyes and looked at each other. "How do you feel?" asked Rowland.

"Excited," said Sam.

"Happy about my new start," said Max. He still hadn't had dessert, and it still didn't matter.

To think about:
Have you ever said a prayer like the one Rowland and Margaret prayed with Sam and Max? If you think the prayer is important why not ask a Christian friend to say it with you? Maybe it would help if they say the words first and you repeat after them.

"Father God, thank you for making me and for loving me. Thank you for sending your only son Jesus to shed his blood and die for me and to take the punishment for all my sins. I am sorry for all I have ever done wrong. Please forgive me and help me to start again. Lord Jesus, I believe in my heart that God raised you from the dead. Please come into my life, be my closest friend and make me new. Please fill me with your Holy Spirit and help me to follow you. Thank you for saving me and for my new start. In Jesus's name, amen."

CHAPTER VII

A Call for Help

Sam and Max's adventure had taken an amazing turn. They had just become Christians on Rowland and Margaret's farm, and were wondering what this new start may mean for them. They gladly accepted Rowland and Margaret's invitation to stay with them a little longer. They remained there for two days, helping Margaret milk the cows and feed the chickens and looking after the horses (Max wanted to make a chariot for them to pull but Margaret wasn't having any of it!). They also did all sorts of jobs with Rowland in the fields, including sheep shearing!

"Jesus once described himself as the 'good shepherd' and said that he would give his life for the sheep," said Rowland. "Most shepherds love their sheep, but not enough to do that! Jesus is different though. He loves every single person in the world and is longing for them to accept him as you two have."

"But why does that make him a shepherd?" asked Sam.

"What do you think a shepherd does?" Rowland asked.

Max spoke up. "Leads the sheep to grass and water, shears them..." he started waving his sword around enthusiastically at the next bit "and protects them..."

"Exactly," finished Rowland.

'So a shepherd pretty much meets every need the sheep has' said Sam, satisfied.

"Absolutely," Rowland chimed. "Jesus once saw a

crowd of people and felt sorry for them because they were like sheep without a shepherd. Everyone needs Jesus to be their shepherd, because he is the way to God and everyone needs to know God. He is that shepherd for you."

During their stay on the farm the boys learned a lot. They were really excited about their new life with Jesus. Rowland taught them some Christian songs and Margaret read the Bible with them, looking in both the New Testament where the book of Romans was but also in the Old Testament, including Psalm 23 which talks about being sheep. She said that one always helped to make sense of the other. Not only were the boys having a wonderful time and growing in their relationship with God but Max's cold got better too. Their quest on the Roman Road was not complete though, as Rowland reminded them once the final sheep had been sheared:

"It's been great to have you young men here, and you are welcome anytime, but your adventure won't complete itself." He put one hand on Sam's shoulder and one on Max's and smiled. Max nodded.

"We need to get back on the road, Sam."

"I know," Sam sighed, "but we have so much to learn, and I guess I'm enjoying myself here."

"You can always come back," Rowland said, "but we have others to explain Romans 10:9 to, and your quest is not over." The boys knew he spoke the truth. That evening was their last on the farm so Margaret made some carrot cake for them and packed them off with food for the last leg of their journey. In the evening they prayed together.

Sam and Max prayed that Rowland and Margaret would be able to help many more people come to know Jesus and they prayed that the boys may be able to share their new life with others on the road.

After a deep night's sleep and a delicious breakfast (Sam had porridge and Max had boiled eggs) the adventurers were on the road again. Unlike when they were on it last time, things were quieter now. There was no one around, and the morning wasn't as bright as it was when they arrived at the farm; in fact it was rather misty. They walked past the big '10:9' they had seen before and carried on ahead, where the sounds of mooing cows grew fainter and Max turned to have one final look at the farm. He couldn't believe what he saw. There, walking into the farm with Rowland and Margaret, was Nash! He was sure of it, even in the mist.

"Sam look quick!" he blurted. "It's Nash going into the farm!"

Sam turned. "What?! No way! What's he doing here!" Sam clenched his fists. "He's not supposed to be here! He's an idiot! What's he doing on this road anyway? We should tell Rowland what he's really like. He's horrible...he's..."

"Like a sheep without a shepherd?" Max tried.

Sam took a deep breath and relaxed. "You're right, Max. We were too before we met Jesus."

"Besides," said Max, "how great would it be if Rowland and Margaret helped him to know Jesus too?"

"Very!" Sam exclaimed, smiling, and he took a moment to say a prayer for him.

"I wonder what has happened to Andrew though."

"No idea," said Max. They walked on into the day, with Sam in front and Max a few steps behind, wondering what adventure they would meet next. It wasn't long before they knew.

"Help!" came a voice on the wind. It was a man's voice. It came again. The boys looked at each other and quickly ran ahead in the direction of the voice. It didn't take them long to get to its source. There was a circle of stones piled in the middle of the road that was as tall as Sam, so naturally Max couldn't see over it without climbing. The cries were ringing out from inside.

"Help! Is anyone out there? Please help me!" came the voice. It was dark inside the circle of stones which turned out to be a well. There was a rope leading into it. The boys looked at each other.

"Hello" said Sam. "Is someone down there?"

"Yes! Please help me!" replied the voice. "I'm stuck down here and can't get out!"

"How did you get down there?" asked Max, suspecting it was some kind of trap.

"I fell! Please — is that Sam and the soldier?" the voice replied. The boys both had open mouths with shock, wondering who the voice belonged to.

"Yes," Sam replied. "But who are you?"

"It's me, Tony" came the reply. "I met you at the signpost a few days ago."

Sam remembered Tony lending him his phone so he could phone his Mum and Grandma. Max remembered the food they had shared.

"Hi Tony!" they both shouted. They were really keen to help now they knew who it was.

"What can we do?" asked Sam.

"There's a bucket down here which feels quite secure. If you pull the rope maybe you can pull me up?" Tony tried.

The boys tried too—they tried pulling the rope as hard as they could, even tying it round Max's waist, but it was no good. All they achieved was rope burn on their hands.

"We're not strong enough" said Sam, deflated. It was hard for even him to admit, let alone macho Max, who chose not to listen and was now grunting like a wild bull in an attempt to pull Tony up by himself.

"It looks like you two need a hand," said a voice from behind them. The boys turned to see Andrew!

"Err, yes, but—hi Andrew," stammered Sam. "How—"

"We can chat later," Andrew said, "but right now I think your friend needs help." Sam nodded.

"Yes! You sure showed up at the right time!" After a few minutes of heaving and straining (not to mention sweating and everyone resisting the urge to let go of the rope for the pain) Tony was free.

"I can't thank you all enough," he said, breathless. He wasn't the only one to feel that way. As he crawled out he noticed all three of them lying on the floor nursing their poor hands.

"Sorry about your hands, fellas," he said.

"S'ok," said Sam. "How did you fall down there?"

"I looked in out of curiosity and saw something very shiny was at the bottom, so I peered in to see but then some stones gave way and I lost my footing."

"Are you hurt?" Andrew asked.

"Surprisingly I'm ok thanks apart from a few grazes."

"Well what was the shiny thing?" said Max.

"Aah, yes," Tony said, looking back to the bucket. "It was this." He held aloft a plaque which he dusted a little to reveal '10:13.'

"Looks like we were meant to go down that well after all," said Max to Sam.

"Yeah, maybe," Sam replied. He then asked Tony and Andrew: "Have you two been reading the Bible?"

"I don't have a Bible remember," Andrew smiled.

"I have and I still don't fully understand everything I've read," said Tony. "Can you help please?"

"Yeah," said Sam, "but how come you are here if you haven't understood them?"

"Well," said Tony, "After you left me at the signpost I decided it was worth carrying on. I realised that I needed to start to trust what God was telling me." The boys nodded.

"So how did Nash end up at the farm?" Sam asked.

"Oh, you saw him go there?" Andrew asked. Max nodded.

"Well, we had a bit of a fall out. He came along as far as the farm but he said he wanted a warm meal and a comfy bed and that he was sick of being on the road, so he went to the farm and that was that. We didn't think he'd want to stick with us if he got what he wanted at the farm."

"I'm sure he will," Sam smiled, winking at Max. "We know the people who own it and they are lovely. He may leave with more than he hoped for!"

"What do you mean?" Andrew asked.

"Well, you were probably wondering what that big 10:9 on the road means? Well, they explained it to us, and let's just say our whole lives have changed!"

"Is this something to do with that eternal life you were dancing about back at the signpost?" Tony asked, unsure what to make of things.

"Yes!" Max blurted. "Romans 10:9! Jesus has given us both a new life and he wants to do the same for you two!"

"Whoa, now this I want to hear," said Tony.

"Yes!" Andrew exclaimed. "When you left Nash and I you were talking about Romans 5:8. Please explain to me what I've missed."

"Gladly! But how did you see 5:8?" Sam asked. "I saw it in a dream..."

Tony replied. "Ah yes, I saw a couple of signs..."

"Fair enough," said Sam. So it was that he and Max told them all about their adventure thus far. Starting with how they had come to be on the road, how they had met, and how God had guided them and looked after them. They explained that Romans 5:8 spoke of Jesus dying for them because of God's great love even though everyone does things which make God sad, and they also explained Romans 10:9 and the need for everyone to know Jesus as Lord. Sam did most of the talking, and Max chipped in on the rare occasions when Sam stopped to take a breath! They were so excited as they told of their friendship with Rowland and Margaret, and how they had helped them to find a new life with Jesus. Andrew was lapping up their every word, and Tony the deep thinker was listening closely.

"I'm glad we saw you again, Tony," said Sam. "And you, Andrew."

Max laughed. "Well, read it then!"

"Oh yeah!" said Sam. "10:13!" Sam dug his Bible out and flicked to the verse. "Romans 10:13 says, "Anyone who calls on the Lord will be saved"."

"That makes enough sense," said Max.

"Is that how you would describe what has happened to you?" Tony asked.

"Well, yeah!" said Sam. "We are saved from trying to live our own way if we put our trust in Jesus and follow him. He has already taken the punishment for all our mistakes and he helps us to have a relationship with God. According to this verse, everyone who calls on his name will be saved from a life without God. That is just the best news ever!"

"Please help me," Andrew pleaded. "I want this new life that you have!" Max smiled and said:

"We have seen some big changes in you already, but the best is about to come!"

"What about you Tony?" Sam asked.

"I'm just thinking about what happened in the well. I'd been in there a good hour before you came. If I hadn't asked for help—and if you three weren't here, I wouldn't have been saved," said Tony.

"You don't say," replied Sam sarcastically. That was when the Bible verse made sense, and looking around Tony could tell that everyone understood, including himself.

"Well, boys, I don't know if you are going to dance again, but..." everyone looked at him intently.

"I'm in." Tony's expression went from one of warmth to one of shock, as he was greeted by three high-pitched 'whoops' from all around him. Sam linked arms with Andrew and started spinning around, and Max banged his sword on his shield and cried out in delight. This was the best moment Sam and Max had experienced

since they had been on the road. Becoming Christians was an amazing highlight for them but to see Tony again, to make friends with Andrew and to help them meet Jesus too—words couldn't describe their excitement. Tony did not join in the dance, but you could tell that if he did he would dance like somebody's Dad. When things had calmed down he asked:

"So what do we do now? Do we pray or something?"

"Yup," said Max. Sam tried to remember the prayer that Rowland and Margaret had prayed with them, with Andrew and Tony repeating after them like they had done. It was a great moment, followed by Tony getting out his camping stove and cooking them a meal, and the boys sharing their carrot cake from the farm. Tony was his usual quiet self as Andrew talked a lot about the decision they had just made and how it would affect them.

"Basically, we are all like sheep," said Max. "Every person is." Andrew looked rather puzzled at him, awaiting an explanation.

Sam knew where he was going with this as Max continued, "We all have to choose if we want to follow Jesus. You just did, and now you never have to be alone!"

"Or afraid," Sam added, then he showed Andrew and Tony Psalm 23.

"Cool!" Andrew said. "I wonder where this road leads though, and how much further we have to go."

"We'll have to get you a Bible when we get home and maybe we can read it together," said Sam. "Are you carrying on with the road then?"

"Yes. My life has changed a lot so far and it seems a shame to turn back now," Andrew replied.

"Aye," said Tony. "We can't be too far from the end."

"There's only one way to find out," said Max, and after they'd eaten they got up and kept walking. Though they didn't know it the end of the road was almost in sight, and the biggest challenge of all awaited them. The boys had some good friends journeying with them, Max was sure to be accepted as a proper Roman soldier and Sam was close to receiving some armour too, though he had no idea what for. With Jesus as their shepherd though, they knew that they had nothing to fear.

To think about:

Read Psalm 23. What do you think about King David's description of God being like a shepherd? Have you let Jesus be your 'good shepherd' like Sam and Max and their friends?

After everything Nash had done, it was hard for Sam to see him going to Rowland and Margaret's house. Why was Sam wrong to react the way he did?

Do you know people like Andrew or Tony who need help understanding what Jesus has done for them? What can you do to help them understand the good news of Jesus?

CHAPTER VIII

At the End
of the Road

Two friends had become four as Sam, Max, and now Tony and Andrew made their way along the Roman Road. Sometimes they walked as a four all in a line, but most of the time they walked in twos as conversations started and stopped. Max was much more relaxed than ever before now the others were with them and didn't see himself needing his weapons again. Still, every time they stopped he would polish his armour, breathing on it and then giving it a rub. He wanted Rome to be proud of him when the adventure was over. Everyone was thinking about how much farther they would have to walk and how it would look when they got there, but no one wanted to say what they thought the end would be like. The road went up again from here. Gulls could be heard somewhere nearby, but all that could be seen up ahead were trees. The road was coming to a halt.

"So this is it," said Sam. "The end of the road." All was silent as they each took in their surroundings. In the middle of a grove of trees there was an aged man sitting at a table. He was by far the oldest man any of them had ever seen. He wore a ragged robe and his beard was long and scraggly. On closer inspection Sam was sure there could have been some crumbs in it. A few yards away was a humble hut which they could only assume was his home. They looked at each other in puzzlement and shrugged. Tony led the way up to the old man, who was writing in a huge weathered book.

"Hello there," he said. The man made no response. Tony walked right up to the table. "I said hello there" he tried again. The man remained with his head down, slowly scrawling onto his page. Tony laughed out of shock, feeling ignored. Andrew wasn't much of a talker, and Max wasn't confident with new people, so it fell to Sam to speak next.

"Hello?" he said. "Sir? Do you speak English?" No response, just slow, laboured writing.

"Maybe he's deaf," Max suggested.

"What's he writing?" Andrew asked. Tony got as close as he felt was polite in order to peer at the book.

"It's all names!" he said. "It's a list."

"Whose names?" asked Sam, getting closer. Tony gasped.

"Our names—and many others!"

"What, all of ours?" Max enquired.

"I can see mine, and Andrew's," Tony replied. "Which book is this, mister, and how do you know our names?" he demanded of the writer. The old man slowly lifted his head.

"Romans 12:2," he said faintly, looking down again to write.

"I think he said Romans 12:2," said Andrew.

"You know what to do, Sam," said Max. Out came the Bible and he read the verses aloud. They said:

"Do not change yourselves to be like the people of this world, but be changed within by a new way of thinking. Then you will be able to decide what God wants for you; you will know what is good and pleasing to him and what is perfect."

They reasoned that the names in the book were people who had chosen to follow Jesus and so had chosen to live his way instead of the ways of the world. Andrew had found Max's and Sam's names in there whilst they were reading the Bible. Resigned to the fact that they wouldn't get any more out of the old man, when Tony said: "So what now?" everyone wondered what they would do next. Where would they go now they had reached the end of the road? And how would being a Christian impact the rest of their lives? It had felt like a bit of an anticlimax to Sam. He was sure they were missing some sort of clue or sign which would guide them in what to do next. He could hear conversation going on all around him. Tony wanted to return to his home, Andrew wanted to go back and see how Nash was and Max wanted to stay there until he became a Roman soldier, or at the least ensure he accompanied Sam home safely. Sam would know all of this if he'd been listening, but he'd zoned out from the voices some moments ago. He was looking at the old man, whom he was certain was looking straight back. Nervously Sam had redirected his gaze several times, but every time he looked back at the man he was met by the same pair of narrow eyes. Sam wanted to talk to him but didn't think he would get a response. Wanting to know why he was being stared at, and knowing staring to be rude, he walked closer. He went almost as close as he'd been before, and as he stood still he noticed the man looking down at the table. Sam's eyes followed. The man had stopped writing altogether; in fact his pen lay still near the big book. Sam looked across to the man's writing hand, which lay spread flat, palm down. It was completely motionless save for the pointing finger, which was tapping up and down. Sam wondered what the purpose was. Perhaps the man was taking a rest from writing. Perhaps there were no new names for the book at that moment. Or perhaps he was trying to draw Sam's attention to the 'Romans 10:14-15' that was etched into the wood. Sam jumped with excited surprise as he suddenly realised what he'd seen:

"Huh?! Hey guys come over here!"

"Thank you," he said to the old man, who laughed, picked up his pen again and carried on as before.

"What's happened?" asked Max, arriving just before the others.

"Look at this," Sam said, showing everyone the writing. "I can't believe we didn't notice this before." Sounds of shock came from Max and Tony.

"Well, what does it say?" asked Andrew.

"Good question!" Sam smiled, digging out his Bible. "Just a sec," he said, thumbing through the pages. "Romans 10:14-15 says: "Before people can ask the Lord for help, they must believe in him; and before they can believe in him, they must hear about him; and for them to hear about the Lord, someone must tell them; and before someone can go and tell them, that person must be sent. It is written, "How beautiful is the person who comes to bring good news.""

Sam looked at the wooden cross around his neck and asked God to help him understand. He thought about the verse. "How beautiful..." he muttered, "is the person..." Sam didn't consider himself beautiful and thought that was a girly word anyway, but he looked down at himself. As he was looking at his feet and thinking "What's so special about me anyway?" he began scanning the floor around them. Walking just a little farther ahead he discovered that beyond them was the sea at the bottom of a rather short cliff, which he'd had no idea about until now.

He looked down to see a narrow, pale beach. The tide was gently lapping in and out of the shore, and just in front of it stood a person, looking back up. Sam could not believe what he saw. It was his Grandma! Finding a nearby dirt path he ran down to her as fast as his legs could take him. Just like on his birthday (which felt like years ago) he ran to her as fast as he could and arrived out of breath, though thankfully he wasn't full of food this time. She embraced him at the bottom as Max caught up to them.

"Well done, Dearie! I knew you would make it," she said in delight, squeezing him as tight as her slight frame would allow. "And as for you, young Maximus! Come here!" She pulled Max into what became a three way hug. Tears flowed down her cheeks and Sam fought back some of his own. They were happy tears of course but no young man wants to cry in front of his Grandma.

"Are your names in the book?" she asked. Sam and Max nodded.

"What are you doing here Grandma? I don't quite understand," said Sam. She began to explain as Andrew and Tony arrived on the scene.

"Many years ago I made this journey myself," she smiled. "I came back for you in the car, as my parents did for me. Now that your journey is complete boys I must take you home Samuel. You must say goodbye to your friends now, unless they want to come too." Sam looked around at Max and his newer friends Tony and Andrew. He was happy to see his Grandma and looking forward to seeing his Mum again, and though he knew that Andrew and Tony wouldn't come with them he didn't want to

say goodbye to them just yet, and some things were not quite clear to him.

"What does the verse mean, Grandma, about hearing and bringing good news? Also, you said your parents brought you back from here. Does that mean you brought Mum back from here too?"

"Very good questions, Samuel," she said. "And the answers are linked!" His face lit up as she continued, "People need to hear the good news of Jesus, and they will only hear if those who have heard it are willing to tell them! You have all made the biggest and best decision you will ever make. Your Mother walked this road years ago but sadly didn't get very far. It is up to people like us to share Jesus with those who do not know him or they will miss out on the life they were created for."

"So that's why we need to go back now—for Mum?"

"Yes, Samuel, and others."

"Then let's go!" He was excited now, knowing what he needed to do. Noticing Max looking downcast, he asked him what was wrong.

"I'm really glad we got here Sam but I feel like something is missing." Sam couldn't believe he'd forgotten about Max's dream.

"Oh yeah! You were supposed to become a proper soldier here weren't you?"

"Yes, and I thought you were meant to receive some armour too?" Max said to Sam inquisitively.

"Don't worry, boys," said Grandma. "You have done very well to get here, and I promise you that if you come back with me now all will be explained." Grandma's assurance was good enough for Sam and Max so they said their goodbyes to Tony and set off. It turned out that Rowland and Margaret were old friends of Grandma's so she was happy to drop Andrew off near their house to be reunited with Nash.

"Not everyone will choose to follow Jesus," said Grandma after they'd dropped Andrew off, "and some take much longer than others to decide. We don't know what this Nash boy will choose, but it's his friends—people like Andrew, who will be able to tell him and show him that there is a better way to live."

The journey back to Sam's house took a good few hours. During that time hardly a word was said. The heating was on in the car, Grandma was contentedly humming along to herself and the boys, tired after all they had been through, slept for much of the way. After a while Grandma woke them.

"Here we are, Dearies," she said, the car now stationary. Sam was home. Groggily waking up they left the car to see his Mum excitedly coming to greet them.

"Welcome home, Samuel," she said, giving him the kind of hug Grandma had done a few hours earlier and adding a kiss. "And welcome back, Maximus," she said, giving him a similar greeting. It was good to be home. They went into the house and Sam poured some juice for himself and Max, then they all sat down to talk.

"How was your journey?" Mum asked. "I was worried about you and am so glad

your Grandmother found you."

"You needn't have been, Mum," said Sam. "Max and I were safe all the time. We made some great friends, and the Bible Grandma gave me has helped to change both our lives!"

"What do you mean?" Mum asked, concerned.

"He means they reached the end," said Grandma. Mum looked at the boys in shock.

"You made it to the end? You mean you understood the Bible verses, and you—"

"—Yes, Mum," Sam continued, "We are both Christians. It's ok—we have really thought about the decision we made and we have been given a new start. Jesus has become our friend and changed us, and he wants to be your friend too!" Mum was deep in thought, smiling politely but her mind was all over the place. "Mum I think you need to get back on the road again," said Sam.

"You may be right," she said. "Perhaps I will, if you can help me understand some of the Bible verses." Sam smiled in optimistic delight and gave her a hug. Grandma winked at him as though to say "well done". Max, suitably refreshed from the juice and his glass now empty, seized his opportunity:

"Why didn't I become a proper soldier? And where is Sam's armour?"

"Ah yes" she said. "Now is the time. You thought you were going to become a proper soldier when you finished your journey." Max nodded. "And you will! But not a Roman soldier." Max's face dropped. "And your armour will be the same as Sam's, for you are now soldiers in the same army!" Sam and Max exchanged glances. Sam was smiling a little; Max was just confused.

Grandma said, "You may think that the journey you are on is over but really you are still at the beginning. There are sixty-five more books in the Bible than the book of Romans and there is so much more for you to see and learn as you grow closer to God. There is some special armour that God wants you to wear which will help you to follow him."

"Oh cool, Grandma! Is it like Max's?" asked Sam.

"No, Dearie," she replied.

"What kind of armour is it then? I want to wear it right now!" Sam impatiently spurted.

Smiling, his Grandma replied, "I love your enthusiasm, Samuel. Now, let's just calm down and I will tell you all about it."

"Can we have cake?" Max grinned. Food always lifted his spirits.

"Yes, Maximus" she sighed and smiled, "We can have cake."

"Thanks!" he exclaimed. So it was that Sam, his Mum and Max all sat round listening attentively to what Sam's Grandma was going to say. With cake in their

mouths and excitement in their hearts, they listened as she spoke:
"Now the armour of God..."

To think about:

Do you have friends or family who will encourage you on your journey of faith? How can they help you, and how can you encourage others?

With Romans 10:14-15 in mind, do you think it is worth sharing Jesus with others even if not everyone will choose to follow him? How do you think you could do this?

Would you like to hear about how the armour of God helps you to live as a Christian? If so, why not ask a Christian friend to explain it to you, or look it up in the Bible in the book of Ephesians chapter 6 verses 10-18?